Alien Ally

Michael A. Susko

Published by AllrOneof Us Publishing, 2020.

This is a work of fiction. Similarities to real people, places, or events are entirely coincidental.

ALIEN ALLY

First edition. August 30, 2020.

Copyright © 2020 Michael A. Susko.

ISBN: 978-1393962779

Written by Michael A. Susko.

Table of Contents

This book is dedicated to those who dream of other worlds and sometimes inhabit them.

Chapter I
Some Madness to Survive

Cast off from a fleet, I was a lone survivor of a medium battle-class ship. The rest of the crew left by escape pods. It was a clever ruse by the enemy, hacking our systems, making the captain believe that the ship's destruction was imminent. Now the enemy has their pickings of defenseless pods while the warship would await empty, ready to be converted to enemy use.

They did not count on me though, one who wasn't taken in. I'd been an expert in gaming before going on a real warship, and I could tell that the patterning, while close to actuality, had a whiff of the artificial, a gamesters' flair. My observation didn't make it to the Captain, for the first officer asked for my evidence. I had none. "We can't operate on a hunch," the first officer said. "Find your escape pod if you value your life."

"Check first with the other ships," I begged. "See if there's the same pattern."

"No time," said the officer, signing off. So I stayed on board and survived. Space became filled with the crew pods destroyed by precise enemy fire.

On inactive status, in a special chamber which insulated my life readings, I played dead. It would take some time before they checked this ship, as it was on the fleet's periphery. Before then, I would have to make a run for it.

One person operating and defending a ship was a near impossibility. I could steer the ship to try to escape, sure enough, but I couldn't also handle weapons. Or, I could man the weapons and not operate the ship.

My demise was just delayed, but at least this would be one ship the enemy wouldn't get.

The question was when to make the move. Systems were all operable. The hyper-drive was ready. The ship could almost disappear, but it would leave traces and would be followed and found. A single ship wasn't worth much, but I was aware of their ruse.

A second problem occurred to me. Far from my home planetary system, the ship depended on refueling from another ship or planetary source. I would have to stop in unknown sectors for help. A warship with a single life form would be suspect as a suicide mission, disease ridden, or even a planet destroyer. Any reasonable planetary defense system would destroy the ship first, then ask questions. We had a state-of-the art, computerized translator that could decode languages, but it would take too much time.

Perhaps it would be better to drift into space and enjoy what time I had left. I considered what to do for the next few moments and decided to de-stress for a while. In the 360 surround holotype with wrap-around visuals, sound, and smells sent by the winder, I put the setting on relaxation, and found myself floating among clouds.

I was only an hour in deep mode, when a sound startled me, and I knew I had miscalculated. The ship had been boarded. They could have worked as well from the outside in... I debated whether I should resist, or just enjoy the rest of the digital trip. Perhaps I would be overlooked. The enemy would be thorough, no doubt, so I decided to go out and meet my fate.

When I opened the holotype door, I met a shielded entity pointing a gun at me. I didn't make a move, surprised to see a single person, its expression emotionless, reading death. I thought to myself, Goodbye. Then the expression relaxed, and I recognized the uniform was from our side.

"How did you get on board?" I asked.

She lowered her gun. "A space pod doesn't have much maneuverability. But I figured it out before I hit eject. I managed with small bursts to direct myself to the emergency hatch. It took some time."

"You're lucky I didn't have the shields up."

"I suppose I am."

"I'm glad you've come aboard. I need a gunner."

"What's your rank?" she challenged.

By chance we had the same rank.

"How many years of service?" she asked.

She beat me by a single year, but regulations only gave it a preference.

"I was the second flight officer on my previous ship for a time," I informed.

"Noted."

"What are your specialties?" I queried.

"Survivability, bionic plants and communications."

"Great. Have you ever fired a ship's weapons?"

"No, but I pick up things quickly."

I studied her for a moment. There was confidence I could work with. In any case, it would have to do.

I had my work cut out, as I had only two rotations in ship weaponry. I was surprised that she picked up concepts and instrumentation quick enough. Her reflexes, however, lagged.

"Did you ever game?" I asked.

"Game?"

I sighed. "You need to start practicing, unless you want to pilot the ship."

"I suppose you're good at that?"

"The first flight officer used to take a lot of time off. I got plenty of flying time in before ..." I don't know why I was about to reveal what happened. Maybe there is an assumed confidence between two survivors. She waited patiently.

"Before my last flight."

She didn't say anything.

"I took a risk. Saved everyone's life though."

"You did?"

"We were outgunned, outnumbered, sure to die if we didn't surrender. It was death or prison planet for the rest of our lives. I went full speed toward the command vessel. It moved aside at the last split second."

"The captain should have given you an award."

"I disobeyed his orders."

"Yes, captains have a thing about that."

"What did he do afterwards?"

"A reprimand and reassignment to a non-piloting position."

"So we have a madman as a pilot?"

I noticed she said we. "Let's go to the simulcast and work on your reflexes," I redirected. "We're going to need some madness to survive."

Chapter II
Energy Anomaly

Judith improved some, though she wasn't a natural. I noted one thing that could prove useful. She did well in high difficulty situations. Somehow she sensed the whole picture and would make the statistically best choice. She would avoid the choice a reasonable person would typically make and succeed. She scored nearly twice my stat.

"You'll do," I said. Her eyes showed disappointment. The truth was she had improved considerably and with time would become competent. But we didn't have time. I tried to console her, made a joke, but it fell flat. I didn't take it personally. Judith had yet to smile. I guessed it was a reasonable response, when you go into survival mode.

We lay dormant for a full day, and I knew that we couldn't risk more. A rough calculation based on a number of ships and projected search time gave us two days. Passive scans were still blank, but once detected it would be nearly too late.

"We're leaving within the hour," I announced. "After a systems check, I'll activate the engines." Then, almost as if on cue, a blip appeared.

"A scout," I cried. "Sealed chamber!" I could only pray that we made it in time. We hastened inside a central cubicle, closed its ultra-thick hatch, turned on the read-out console to monitor the fly by. The alien ship circled, then paused for what seemed like an eternity. We guessed it was deciding whether to board. The standard would be for an expert team to search the ship and make short work of any survivors. But it left and we both exhaled. Probably they boarded random ships, based on certain inputs, and we had won the toss of the die.

"Too easy," Judith said after we stepped out.

I looked at her questioningly.

"They must have noticed something. The computer would have made a quicker decision. They had to think. They noticed an anomaly."

"But they didn't do anything."

"I don't know why. Maybe they're calling for backup. We're a warship, after all. Something bigger is probably close."

"You could be right" I was surprised she might be reading the situation better than I. "So there's no time for run downs or flight checks. Let's go."

The ship hummed to full life, passive scans went active, and I set travel coordinates. Logically, we should just go straight out and away, gaining maximum distance. "What angle?" I threw out. "Forty-five degrees," she replied.

I split the difference. "OK, we'll go straight first, leaving a trail, then turn."

The ship's engine's faint whir signaled readiness. Belted in, we waited three seconds, which always seemed ten times longer than it was. A flash of acceleration, and we vanished temporarily from whatever was tracking us. We went ten seconds before we turned left.

At that point I activated full scans.

"Three ships responding," I noted, keeping my calm. Our turning had not delayed them long. "Projected time till contact, ten minutes." Their ships were faster by some 10%, which was all the difference in battle. We had some edge in maneuverability though, which would keep us alive longer. But three fully manned ships against one with a crew of two were no odds.

"Ready?" I asked.

"Yes," she answered with more confidence than was warranted.

"Remember, don't fixate on hits, whether yours or theirs. Move on to the next shot."

"Got it."

The alien ships closed steadily, and my shipmate queried, "Strategy Mark?"

She used my name. Combat did that, made for a type of intimacy.

"My job is make us a difficult target. Your job, Judith, is to kill three warships. In the end, we survive."

The impossibility of it struck me. A novice might make a lucky kill, but three in a first battle situation was not in the statistical cards.

I would have to rely on some extreme maneuvering skills. I looked ahead to the point of projected space where we were headed, swathes of empty space. No cover. To the left and barely visible, there was a cluster of sorts, clouds with scattered matter. Not much, but we might risk stopping and cloaking there. We had technology that could cloak if there was some ambient matter about, provided they didn't send a direct scan right at where we were in the cloud. I could send ahead a diversion pod that would mirror the ship. It had a chance of fooling them for a short time.

Short term it worked. They did not expect our move and passed wide of us.

I waited a full minute, then suggested, "Direct a seeking neutron bomb right at them."

"Won't they evade it?"

"Set the device to detonate a few moments before they are likely to detect it. It will gain us time."

She fired, and I moved full speed in the opposite direction. Their captains would be surprised. Our ship was supposed to be ahead of them, but now a missile would come from behind them.

We were doubling separation distance. "There's only smooth space," I said, scanning all directions.

"There," she said, looking at her consoles.

"Where?" There was no solid object or cloud on my screen.

"An energy anomaly at 73 degrees."

I turned on my energy scanner, and there it was. "Not typical. More power expected for its size... Protocol is steer well clear of such readings."

"We need help."

She was right again. If the fluctuation were dangerous to us, it would be dangerous to the enemy.

I reset the coordinates. "We're going there. Belt in."

You never know what to expect in anomalous energy fields. When we first entered, there were only faint points of light, the points looking like bits of light spitting, fading suddenly only to reappear. It was an anomaly, one that I hadn't encountered or read about.

"What is it?" I wondered out loud.

"Space is filled with energy. Something's interacting, making it visible."

I reflected on that and wondered what was the second factor. Whatever the cause, it became thick such that our screens looked like a holiday display.

The consoles flashed suddenly brighter, our instruments became erratic for several seconds, and the main engine went off line.

Quickly, I surveyed the readings. "We still have pulse power. What about shields?"

"Down."

"We'll have to fly by eye and unprotected," I said, not believing it. One rarely flew by eye, and our training only covered that as a formality. As for being exposed, we had training, but not in combination with blind instruments.

"It's getting crazy," I remarked.

"That's good," she offered.

"It increases the random factor." I killed the pulse engines, slowing us down. "Whatever this is, we're in pretty deep. Best to wait it out, however. Movement might expose us. I get the feeling it won't be getting better the further we go into whatever this is."

"Something else I'm noting."

I saw nothing on my console. "Other aliens?"

"No, us—our neural fields."

Instinctively, I closed my eyes and sensed my thoughts. They raced, drifted as if going off line, into a dead space. Then back on again in... definitely off-key.

"Yes, I feel it. How is it impacting you?"

"It's making my logical train skip – too fast, then slow, messing with coming to a conclusion."

"Maybe we should get out," I suggested. "Sanity is one thing we can't afford to lose."

"No hope if we go outside this," she said, stating the obvious. "Perhaps we can correct for the distortion."

I turned my thoughts inward, but no logical solution presented. I wondered if the distortion was preventing me.

"There – they're here!" she suddenly cried.

Our ship convulsed. We had taken a hit. An alien ship appeared on our right side. The blast, for some reason, didn't breach the hull. It took me a moment to realize that our ship's close range blasters had fired first. The shaking was the blow back explosion of the destroyed enemy ship pushing us deeper into the energy field.

"Good job," I said, wondering how it was possible.

"I was lucky."

"It wasn't luck," I complimented. She was better than I thought. I instinctively took more risk, moving the ship deeper into the field. Luck would not work against two remaining ships. The energy became brighter as we went further in. My mind felt pulled, taking more effort. "Yes, deeper in--I understand now--the ships are only visible outwards. They didn't see us, even though they were nearly on top of us. But if we go further in--more danger." My mind seemed to reach a danger point, and I stopped the ship. Going further in no longer seemed an option.

The conundrum of the distortion became apparent to me. I considered the best path forward. An answer seemed to come to me, then left.

"It's getting worse," she said, and I saw her face. Pain creased her expression as she tried to hold her mind. But I saw determinedness too. She would be all right for a space.

"Two more out there. Keep alert," I managed to say.

Chapter III
Battle Conundrum

For a period my mind would blank, then perfect clarity would present. *How much further could we go into the anomaly without totally losing our faculties?* I wondered. Somehow I needed to calculate that. We had to see them before they saw us, given our situation. Yet, if our minds were not battle ready...

She seemed to read my conflict. "My vote is to keep going in. We don't know how their organism will react. Whether they or we are more resistant to this stuff."

"There must be a way to trace them without our naked eye," I murmured out loud. We were not specialists in detection, and my mind presented no solution. "Yes, going further in," I decided. I placed the pulse engines on the lowest setting forward.

A few minutes later we seemed to have no worsening of effects. Then two blurs passed by. Two enemy ships had sped forward, oblivious to the danger.

"What do we do now?" I asked. "They'll turn around and detect us first. We won't see them. We're dead."

"Imagine we can," she replied.

"Yes?" I asked, then got it. I steered, imagining I was evading ships, making complicated maneuvers. "This will only work for so long," I realized out loud. "Impulse power will need to recharge."

"How much time do we have?"

"Twenty minutes tops."

"Wait there!" A weapon beam passed through the energy field, narrowly missing us. "It's creating a distortion at the source," she noted.

"Yes, we can track it back and position the ship. But our information might come be too late... They'll be moving." A possible solution presented, but it slipped my mind.

"We could try our high yield bomb right after a read out," she managed to propose.

My adrenalin brought clarity. "Too close. We'd be in within shock range."

"Fire and move away. They'll either have to come into it, or go deeper."

"Possibly. Do it, " I ordered. "We need a new reading." Our ship jolted, providing the answer.

"Do what?" she asked. "Outer bulkhead penetrated, inner holding... Two ships are now attacking."

"Can't you . . ." I couldn't remember. *We were done,* I had enough faculty to realize. By the time our minds came back, the enemy would have moved off coordinates.

"A way..." she said. "I'll write it down."

"You have something to write with?"

"Old habit."

The second hit was glancing, knocked our aft weapons out. We could fire from face side.

"Where are we firing?"

"Read it!" I cried.

She looked down, put in the coordinates and fired. "Move outward, outward!"

I didn't remember why, but I did what she said. 100% thrust, risky, but there was no mistaking the urgency in her voice.

"Brace, brace!" she yelled.

Five seconds later, our ship flipped like we were on a roller coaster. Then silence.

"We made a hit," she stated matter-of-factly. "All weapons off line, though." The surprise showed in her voice that we were still there at all.

"Wait... Pulse engines off line as well. We're drifting. Life support is on auxiliary power. We are effectively disabled. The other ship must be near."

We waited for what seemed like an interminable time, when the glittering enemy ship approached, a few degrees to our left.

"We got two," I said, making the best of it.

"Maybe this one's damaged."

"Looks like a complete hull. We almost made it."

"I suppose there's a self-destruct protocol."

"Reasonable option." I pulled out a panel. "At least our minds our coming back."

My hand was coding the sequence when she asked, "Why?"

I couldn't remember. I looked up, saw the enemy ship.

"No, wait. Life readings?"

I did. There were none. "How?" I wondered.

"Not sure. Maybe they went too far into the anomaly and the energy field weakened their minds. Then the explosive wave on top of that, finished them off."

"Doesn't matter why. We live to fight another day."

"Auxy is only good for a few days."

"A problem for later..."

"You did well for your first battle," I remembered to compliment. The effects of the energy anomaly were wearing off. I realized that our situation was dire, our survival chances next to nil. But it felt good to win the battle."

"Didn't do that much," she said. "You did some fine evasion against invisible ships."

"You held your sanity longer than me, and your pen and paper came in handy."

Judith nodded, and a smile traced her face.

Chapter IV
Alien Ship

The explosion of the enemy ship pushed us out of the core of the energy field, and soon we were drifting into standard space. The alien ship remained within viewing range, drifting with the same momentum. I raised the question of boarding the ship, but Judith was not keen.

"Too many unknowns, from possible contaminates, to how to repair and run an alien ship. I don't know if would increase our chances of survival."

"Can't be much worse," I replied. "But we have time to decide. Let's take a break. It's been forever since we've had a meal."

Space fare wasn't gourmet, but passable. It didn't help that we didn't know the tricks of the trade that a cook would bring. Thinking of the cook suddenly caused me to feel a wave of grief, something that survival mode had shunted aside. The loss of the crew crashed upon me like a painful weight. The grief was mixed with guilt, wondering why I hadn't felt it earlier. I suppose one doesn't grieve when your own death looks imminent.

Judith saw my face. "I know," she said. She placed her hand on my shoulder, touching me for the first time. "We lost a lot of friends."

After a meal in mostly silence, I stepped away. "I need to be myself," I said. "Let's decide what to do the start of the next day cycle."

"Any chance of getting the engines on-line?" I asked on the next designated morning. "The core engines are thoroughly dead. The energy field, by whatever means, has fried its inner components.

"Not my expertise," she needlessly said. "I can stretch survivability."

"How long?"

"Maybe two weeks…"

"Well, nobody will find us. A death watch…"

"She turned to the window, staring out. The alien ship was still in view. The question was obvious.

"We should take the risk, even if there are many unknowns." Her statement was half a question.

I looked at her and nodded slightly. "There will be no one to let us in. And the doors won't open from the outside. We'll have to use precision explosives."

"Risky?" she ventured.

"Not in itself. But breaching the hull is not a great way to ready our escape ship." I already doubted the decision. "Maybe another way will present. We could try the holograph. If we take a step away, the answer might come to us."

Her survivability instinct kicked in. "The holodeck isn't good for crisis situations. While you're there, you'll relax too much and think things are normal. When you come out, reality will double down."

That was a long explanation by her standards, and I guessed she was right. The holodeck, in this case, would lesson our chances of survival.

"We'll still need a plan. Over dinner, then. We'll go in tomorrow, after another sleep cycle."

Our dinner was mostly in silence. She wasn't given to small talk. A lot weighed on us. Suddenly I asked her something personal. "Do you have any brothers or sisters?"

She looked at me as if I had broken a rule. "My brothers and sisters were those on this ship."

I gathered she had been sent away early to training, had not much of a childhood. Yet I took some heart, for it made me a brother.

Boarding had not been easy, I reflected, as we walked down the alien ship's corridor. We had been about to give up, as the ship showed no signs of entryway. We ended up placing explosives at what seemed to be a random spot––one Judith selected––and got lucky. The explosive wave did not radiate, popping out a small section. I wondered how she had guessed, but that question would have to wait.

Inside, the angles and lighting––still on––were geared to a different visual field, and like a trick mirror, things appeared out of place. It took a while to adjust.

We moved toward what felt like the center of the ship, though we were aware that our conceptions might not work. Our guns were drawn, although our scanners showed no life forms.

"No bodies," commented Judith, putting up her weapon. "They must have gone somewhere."

The command center filled with instrumentation devoid of any presence. Surprisingly, some display panels showed active, shifting geometric patterns. We examined the instruments, unreadable, and opened some panels, looking for clues.

"They must have evacuated," said Judith. "Still, it doesn't figure..."

"Would they have risked the energy anomaly, as escape pods wouldn't be shielded,"

"Maybe they evaporate when they die."

"Or maybe they teleported to another ship, like in the ancient Star Trek," I threw out.

"That's one thing biological species will never be able to do."

"There's another possibility," I ventured. "This could be a remotely controlled ship. It could be that we're being watched."

"By who?" asked Judith, opening a tall narrow door.

I didn't respond for my attention was held by an upright, oval cannister, its front transparent. Within stood an alien––suspended and motionless––no more than the size of an eleven-year-old. Its body was obscured by a gauzy film, a colorful, liquid crystalline sheen. Definitely bipedal, human enough like, but its detail was blurred behind the gauze and colors.

"We have a survivor after all!" Judith exclaimed.

"Do we?" I asked. "I'm running a scan... this is odd. No sign of life or death. It's got to be one or the other..."

"A third is possible," said Judith. "Aestivation, near death. Animals use it to wait out inhospitable periods. Micro-organisms can remain frozen for decades."

"Not a microorganism here," I said, reaching out to the shield.

"Don't touch! It might drop the shield and activate the alien."

I drew back. "All right. But isn't that what we want?"

"Maybe." Judith considered. "But let's take time to think this through and consider what we're dealing with. Plus, if we activate inappropriately..."

"It looks human-like enough."

"If you can count being four feet tall, with pulsing colors on its surface."

"It appears harmless. No weapons inside. How do we activate an alien organism in aestivation?"

"Standard protocol would quarantine for months. But we will have to speed things up, like immediately. This is actually our best hope. Someone who knows the ship."

"Agreed," I said, listening to my logical mind.

Judith hesitated. "Still, I can think of at least ten risks."

"Tell me the top three. I don't want to be overwhelmed."

"One, we fail to activate the creature, and it dies. Then we're back to where we started. Two, we successfully activate the creature and it succeeds in convincing us or forcing us to go back to its world, a not so friendly place."

I tried to keep positive. "Not great, but we'd live longer. Maybe we'd be placed in a zoo with all our needs are met. What's the third?"

"The alien is friendly and helps us to go home. We'll need to offer something in exchange though, which would present a challenge. One thing has been consistent with alien encounters. An exchange of gifts."

"I'll take the third possibility. We'll come up with something to give the alien, then go back to earth, and we'll live together happily ever after."

"Together?" she asked with an ample measure of disbelief.

I held up my hands, surprised by the hurt I felt. "No need to read anything in. But we've decided? You're the communication expert. How do we do it?"

"The answer is likely somatosensory. We place hands on the shield, and our electrical fields activates the life sequence."

"Yours or mine?"

"Let's start with one hand of each of ours. The alien will know then that we each helped it survive, so it won't just become bonded to one."

"I wouldn't want to lose an edge."

"You can't say I'm not looking out for you." Another smile crossed her face.

It soothed the earlier rejection, and I focused my attention on the alien capsule. "Any special way to place our hands?"

"Palms outward and think with friendly energy."

"Do we say anything like 'Open sesame?'"

"Whatever your good vibe is…"

We each put a hand on the shield. At first nothing happened, then it seemed like we joined each other, the energy between us and within the capsule. Then we experienced too much energy, like a vibrating electrical current, and disengaged.

We looked at each other, differently. "It's uncanny, like we were melding," said Judith.

I nodded, trying to take in what I had just felt.

"Perhaps a gift of the alien," Judith considered. "A good sign…"

"It didn't work though."

"No. Our energy was building, becoming more transparent, not enough to activate. Perhaps if we used both our hands and held on longer."

"Are you sure about this? What if we end up dying to bring this alien alive?"

Judith nodded, recognizing that by melding we became vulnerable.

"There's not much choice," she said softly.

"All right, here goes." I took the lead, placing hands on the shield toward the head of the alien. She put her hands on the upper torso, where the heart might be.

No movement at first, then we missed when it happened. The alien was looking at us with unblinking eyes.

Chapter V
The Animated Alien

Using both of our hands doubled the intensity and unity of our electrical fields. The gauzy envelope became clear, and the outer Mache on the alien dissipated. Within the opening capsule, the clear outlines of the creature appeared, in most respects human-like. Aside from certain off-key, facial angles, one major difference did present. The alien's skin exhibited waves of changing color, in some form of energetic pulsing. It was mainly shades of mauve, shifting between lighter and darker tones.

"No aggressivity so far," noted Judith. "And it looks like an advanced species."

"More colorful... I wonder what sex it is."

Judith didn't respond, for the alien had changed color with our comments. It was subtle, a sudden purple cast, before the calming red-mauve returned.

Next and again, to our surprise, the alien uttered a syllable, which we took as a greeting. Movement followed, slowly stepping out of the capsule, surveying the scene, and taking in the situation more fully.

The being's second utterance, "Thank you." We were perhaps even more surprised at hearing words we understood than the animated alien.

"How do you know our language?" I asked.

"Though on the galactic fringe, your world has been monitored for some time. All deep space travelers are required to know languages operative within their zone."

I tried to dampen my surprise. "That makes sense."

"How many languages in your zone?" Judith queried.

"A half dozen, though not all are normal languages."

There followed a moment when we all looked at each other in silence.

The being appeared to be reading us. "Forgive me for being a bad host. Let us have some food and converse."

In an adjacent room we were seated at a long white, oval table whose chairs had no discernable legs.

Waving my hand underneath the chair, I asked the obvious.

"The physics is not complicated," the alien answered, placing food before us. "Repelling magnetism does the work."

We quickly turned to the food, which appeared to be a fruit-vegetable hybrid. "Delightful," said Judith after a few bites. "I can't quite place the taste."

"Sweet and sour mixed with something else..." I offered.

"We'd like to know more about you," asked Judith, after introducing ourselves. "It would help to know your name and sex, how you like to be addressed."

"Oh yes, the matter of names and sexes," the alien considered, as if searching a file on our species.

"My name was RB-53, while others were on this ship. We avoid the personal on missions when fatalities are likely."

"Your real name, then?" I asked.

"I haven't established my new name yet," the aliens answered, its colors darkening. "Our names change with each cycle, and when there's a significant life change."

"It won't be a problem if you change your name. There are only three of us here," Judith allowed. "What is your sex?"

"In that we differ from humans as well. We are composites, our emphasis shifting."

"You weren't born one way or the other?" I asked.

"The moment of birth is not the deciding factor," the alien answered.

Wanting clarity, I pursued, "What are you now?"

"Today, it is in between. It's better to be neutral when encountering a new species."

"So we can refer to you as *it*?" Judith queried.

"The impersonal pronoun will suffice," answered the alien.

It seemed rather remarkable that we harmonized so readily. The alien had the similar desire to return home, and its ship was salvageable, or so it said. The plan it ultimately presented was to return to its home planet, some ten times closer than earth, then send us on our way. As for what had happened in the recent past, the alien thought fit to offer an explanation. We had inadvertently entered a neutral zone, when a warship detected us and judged us a threat.

I decided to not waste time and acknowledge the elephant in the room. "Was your response justified, to eliminate an entire fleet for an inadvertent trespass?"

"One of your ships opened fire on our command vessel. It missed, destroyed another ship. Our protocol is to eliminate when command vessels are targeted." The alien's color had intensified as it spoke, the mauve shifting to scarlet.

"Yes, I remember, a ship in your advance section."

"The commander of our fleet was on that ship."

I didn't argue any further. We could easily have done the same. I was relieved also to find there had been a reason. Yet the response was not balanced, for they had also eliminated defenseless escape pods.

"It was not my decision," said RB-53, reading me. "I would have not destroyed them. Still, how could you know whether one was real, a decoy, or a bomb?"

I didn't question further, but again felt relief. Morality is a constant in the universe, and our alien friend was no exception. Additionally, combat decisions are to be judged in the context where a split second can make the difference between life and death.

We returned to the immediate issue of making repairs to the alien ship. To this end RB-53 went to work immediately. He appeared competent and was able to answer our questions with authority, though not always within our comprehension. We were given small tasks, mostly checking and cleaning equipment, which left us puzzled as to the underlying principles.

We studied the alien. Its speech was sparse and seldom revealed its inner state. Yet, emotions seemed to be revealed by its colors. As Judith observed, it may have balanced out its tendency not to use many words. We were at some disadvantage, as this was our first up-close, personal encounter with this alien.

In a private moment, I raised the matter with Judith. "So far I have no reason to doubt the alien's intentions. How about you?"

"Can't say," she safely answered. "It's best to keep interacting and see if we can read its patterning of colors. See if there are signatures for truth, falsehood, or something in-between. So far, I'm not getting a negative vibe. And even if we did, we wouldn't have much choice. RB-53 holds all the cards. He alone knows the vessel. A promise of going to a planet offers a far greater probability of survival than being stranded in space."

"Agreed... Still, I wonder why it appears so willing to help. I can't forget that our crew mates were shown no mercy. Do you think we have the full story?"

"Most likely the alien is telling the truth," Judith discerned. "It was battle protocol. Perhaps the alien's actions are also a protocol. Or maybe it's returning a favor. We did bring it back to life."

"We need to keep our eyes open. I'd rather make a move against a single alien than an entire planet."

Lowering her voice, Judith warned, "I'd be careful about brooding or doubting too much. I have a feeling the alien reads more than we're aware. Yet if RB-53 wanted to make a move against us, it could have done so by now. I think it's best to take things at face value."

"We're going to need an alien ally to survive," I agreed.

"I have a feeling," Judith added—"it came from a dream––other hostiles will be the problem."

"We're far from any planetary system. Dreams bring out fears."

"That's another survival instinct I've learned. Dreams can serve as an early warning system."

"Any specifics on that warning?" I pursued.

"It was vague. We were captured though."

"Great," I said. "I'll keep my eyes open and my gun ready."

Chapter VI
Parallel Realities

When the ship hummed to life, a wave of relief passed through us. We would go somewhere, our trust placed in an alien, a ship with an unknown power base and unintelligible instrumentation.

"Good job," I complimented Qua452, who informed us of its new name after the ship's activation. "How long will it take to reach your home planet?"

"Two of our lunar months, one of yours."

"That's far away," I surmised, although I did not know the ship's speed.

"A reasonable time, given our drive is only partly functional. But we have sufficient power to make it."

"That's good news," said Judith.

"There remains a problem," the alien qualified. "Our energy supply is limited, and we will have to pass near Epixolin's border."

"Yes?" I asked.

"There shouldn't be a problem. They're unlikely to have constant surveillance beyond the outer perimeter, and it would not be protocol to intercept us. However, if we are detected, and they make an interception, there won't be much we can do to stop them."

If there was any doubt as to the unwantedness of that possibility, the being's forehead darkened with flashes of green-yellow.

Our faces must have shown distress, for Qua added, "As I indicated, it's unlikely."

I was reflecting how much luck played into survival, when Judith raised an obvious consideration.

"Shouldn't we learn how to use the ship's weapons?"

Swirls of purple traced on the alien's temples. "If it comes down to weapons, we'll lose," it informed. "And the ship's weapons are coded for battle crew use only."

"Maybe I could help steer and you operate the weapons" I offered.

"Not possible, unless you knew Xippean fluently and have been trained."

"Maybe there is something we can do," Judith pursued.

"Of course," said Qua. "There are some things..."

We were given things to do, which appeared to be of little consequence, and we took the time to learn oddities about the alien. For one, we never saw it sleeping. Even if we woke in the middle of our sleep cycle, it would be huddled over the ship's instrumentation, making unknown calculations. One time I woke early and found the alien playing what looked like an electronic video game.

"Do you sleep?" I asked.

"Sleep? We go into altered states for brief periods that refresh us."

"How long?" I wondered.

"As much as an earth hour, supplemented by two briefer periods each day."

I recalled those times when we addressed the alien, and it seemed to be somewhere else.

"Do you dream?" I asked.

The alien was puzzled when I described the phenomenon. "I must have overlooked that in my study of your species," it revealed. "These dreams would be useful, however, in drawing connections."

"Connection to what?" I asked.

"To the deeper dimension which runs parallel to this one. It's highly useful if you need to consider a fuller range of possibilities before you settle on one. Spending time where two dimensions intersect is also highly informative."

Though this seemed important information, a wave of tiredness descended over me. It was too early in my morning to be carefully following this. "We need to talk further," I said, excusing myself.

Coincidentally, that morning, I remembered my dream. *Judith, the alien, and I were standing at the bottom of a long cylinder, its walls lit with pale green. An opening appeared far above, a small yellow circle of light. We melded our minds and started to float...*

"Interesting," said Judith, after I relayed my earlier conversation and dream. "We've found out something more about our alien friend. It doesn't have night dreams, yet it immediately understood them. Perhaps Qua has access to dream consciousness during its normal waking state, lessening its need for sleep."

"Logical," I complimented. "I'm glad you have a handle on this alien."

"I wouldn't go that far. Our need to sleep is a disadvantage and puts our survivability at risk."

"In view of that, why do humans need to sleep so much?" I asked, wanting a more expert opinion.

Judith looked carefully at me, perhaps judging my level of comprehension. "There's no single agreed upon theory. A plausible one is that our brain has evolved to such a high energy state, that it needs significant down time to regenerate and to integrate information that our waking consciousness has absorbed."

"Sounds reasonable, but I'm wondering if there's something more."

"As our alien friend suggests, sleep is about survival and other realities. As humans evolved, there was a tension between immediately useful information, and what is necessary for long term survival. This deeper, parallel, what some call spiritual reality, is simultaneously operative. It provides – if we can sense it—the pathway to our long-term evolutionary future."

"But ancient ways of spirituality were laid to rest centuries ago."

"Among the elite and much of the highly educated," Judith corrected. "It's still alive in disparate groups among the multitudes. Beyond the what and how of the universe, there remains the why."

"Does there even have to be a why?" I argued. "Maybe things just are. Focusing on a why – when we don't even know if there is one—can be a distraction."

"But if a why exists, it could prove imminently useful, a clue on the direction we need to go. For the why is always about the future."

"You're getting philosophical on me."

"So? Philosophy has its use. Asking the *why* question is keeping our eye out for the something beyond our current awareness. The future has a habit of surprising us."

"Perhaps the *something more* are planets with unpredictable species."

This was an area of Judith's expertise. "Yes, within each new species, there are traits and capacities we do not expect. For humans, the sleeping species, we dream and insights are granted."

"Speaking of insight, what did my dream mean?"

"Not sure. Maybe hostiles are ahead... The ancient Mayans believed that dreams portend the future."

Perhaps in sync with Judith's premonitions, the alien's demeanor altered in the days ahead. Flashes of erratic colors told us that something was changing. At the end of one lunar month, something seemed to be bothering Qua.

"I wonder if its name is changing again," Judith considered. "Or perhaps its sex is going out of neutral."

When the alien was asked it informed that it was neither. "A name change only occurs when something major happens, not its possibility. As for the sex dimension, it's not so useful to emphasize in survival situations."

We wondered still what the possibility was. Judith returned to the original question.

"I thought I would wait for more developments, but as you wish," replied the alien. "Our ship is being tracked by the Epixolins. The good news is a ship probe has not been sent our way. I have hoped that they won't take the trouble to disturb us, as the ship is outside their claimed space. But I've had to come close enough to leave discretion to their defensive system." The alien's notably darkened. "No visitors to their planetary system have ever returned. We have only received their fragmented messages."

The alien's words raised our anxiety. Judith, ever thinking of survival, asked, "What are the chances for our safe passage."

"Unknown. By now, they'll know that we're a stranded ship with three survivors. There would be no great desire to take our ship, as they keep their own technology."

"So we should be good," I said.

"Uncertain," replied the alien, its colors becoming various. "Three survivors from two different species. That's an anomaly which would raise questions with the Epixolins."

"Perhaps we should open up a channel and dispel their curiosity," suggested Judith.

"Initiating contact might be interpreted as aggression. Only if they hail us... I'm also not taking evasive action, least that be misinterpreted."

I felt helpless. We were just figuring out an alien species when another, possibly hostile one, was being introduced. We refrained from more questions that might further raise our anxieties. But we were left wondering about the fate of those who never returned.

"There is a way to take control if need be," Qua offered the next day cycle. "It's preferred to being captured, and it follows protocol."

The alien had not mentioned the word, which we both guessed. "It's your ship," I granted. "But a code in our species is do all that's possible to survive, if no greater loss of life is at risk."

"We could gain valuable intelligence on a species, if there is an encounter," Judith added.

"Two votes to one, so you carry," said Qua.

Our faces showed surprise, prompting the alien to add, "It's one of our rules."

"We get an equal vote?" I asked.

"Statistically, greater consensus provides a better result. Thus, it is to my advantage to do so."

We both sensed we had gained encouraging knowledge about the alien. But the immediate problem remained.

"When will we know of the Epixolin's decision?" asked Judith.

"In about 13 of your earth minutes, we should be out of their space."

"I hope that's a lucky thirteen," said Judith with a nervous laugh.

On the twelfth minute, we thought we were out of the woods, when the alien spoke. "Funneling."

"What?" we asked.

As if answering, the ship jarred and stalled.

"Any change on your choice?" asked Qua. "They've taken control of the ship."

"What will happen next?" asked Judith.

"Unknown," said Qua.

"Still confirming your choice?" the alien asked again.

"Unknown is better than ending things," was my reply.

"Anything to prepare us?" asked Judith.

"Two cardinal rules in encountering new species," said Qua. "Show no fear and give respect, in that order."

I wanted to ask what these aliens looked like, but stopped short. Sometimes it was best not to know.

Chapter VII
Meld Transport

An unknown time later, we became conscious, standing. We were in the cylinder like in my dream, its greenish hue extending upward nearly as far as we could see. We had no memory of being taken prisoner.

"How did they do it?" I asked.

"Not known, but efficient," answered our alien friend, whose surface mirrored the greenish tinge. "They obviously don't want us to have a memory of the process."

"This doesn't bode well for us," said Judith, "if they can take us with ease at a distance... No wonder no one has ever left them."

"No one from your or my species," the alien corrected. "It's unknown if others have escaped."

"So why are we in this?" I asked.

"My guess is that it's standard procedure, a period of containment to make sure no diseases are present, or hint of mental weapons."

"Mental weapons?" Judith asked.

"Some species, like your electric fish, can direct their bodily energy and send a powerful electrical charge upon contact."

"Something humans – at least ordinary humans—have never learned to do," I informed.

"That's good," informed the alien. "Such skills would only hurt us here."

"So what do you recommend, Qua–"

"Swaz42," the alien corrected. "As for your question, I have no recommendation."

"We're just going to do nothing?" I asked with impatience. "In my dream we floated up. Can you help us to do that?"

"Oh yes, the meld. . . . We could send out what you call your *dream body*."

"What do you mean?" asked Judith.

"It's a double of yourself, while your real body remains behind."

"It would prove useful to see the lay of the land," I reflected, not quite believing it possible.

"Granted," said Swaz, "but it does present risks. If you leave your body too long, you might not be able to wake upon return. For another, we risk upsetting our hosts."

"I understand that our hosts might become upset, if you can call this hosting," said Judith, "but why is there a risk in leaving the body too long?"

"A body can only live so long with its 'dream body' absent. Then too you might forget to return to your body, or even that you have one, the longer you stay away."

"It feels that real?" Judith doubted. "So, how long is it safe to stay away?"

"Three days in your biological cycle."

"Surely we can stick to that," said Judith. "Shall we do it?"

"We vote again," Swaz replied. "I'm abstaining, for I see no clear direction."

"I'm for it," voted Judith. "Mark?"

"We might wait and see if aliens contact us. But Judith, you're the expert in survivability. Would this hurt or help us?"

"To survive, we need information. Right now we have very little. Imprisoned in a featureless chamber puts us at a considerable disadvantage."

"Then I voted for a limited look-see. No more than a day. . . . lest we upset our alien hosts."

As if on cue, Swaz42 yellowed and brightened.

"Prepare for the meld," it said.

We melded first. It was similar to the alien's awakening, when we felt joined to each other, except this time we united with the alien consciousness. That was hard to describe, like a different color you have never seen before, or a sound you never heard, one that was like human and yet quite human. There was also something more specific. Swaz42 was able, by mental means, to tap into a power reservoir sufficient to raise us, or at least our consciousness upward. Though a dream body, we could view below us our natural bodies in outline form. This separation from our bodies was scary, though I sensed a strict discipline behind the alien's use. At the same time, I felt that such power, if weaponized, could be very dangerous. I wondered, too, if there was also a risk, one that Swaz42 had alluded to, in upsetting our hosts.

As we rode, an uncanny feeling of lightness pervaded us, as if we had been freed from matter and no longer needed our bodies. *This is dangerous,* I found myself thinking.

"Stay together," Swaz42 directed. "It takes time to master movement in this form."

Gradually we rose towards the opening, which became larger and larger, testifying how deep we had been. When we arrived, the immense cone and its summit were perfectly smoothed, suggesting a novel technology had crafted it at one piece.

Judith was looking at me questioningly, this melding not fitting into any of her normal mental categories. "Are you sure we haven't died?" she asked at one point.

I laughed, though part of me knew this was a reasonable question. "If we've died, then that means our consciousness has somehow survived. I'll take that as good news."

"Nothing like this in any of my survival training..."

"We'll have to learn as we go," I suggested. "Flexibility – no doubt they taught you that."

"Too many unknowns," she worried. "All I can say is that it's a good thing we have our alien friend."

I glanced over to Swaz who showed awareness of all we said, and perhaps our thoughts as well. The meld involved a type of joining and transparency whose limits I did not sense. I felt too that I intimately knew Judith, able to guess what she would say before she would say it. As for the alien, we grasped it some better too, though I sensed there remained shielded portions.

We had paused at the rim, sensing that we were about to emerge into a vast hidden world.

When we did, we looked down at the coned mountain which revealed as sculpted by intelligent hands. Its surface was barren of vegetation and not smooth like the interior, but fractled with geometric shapes, suggesting it was formed by another whole set of rules. As for the land below, it was shaped as well, but we were too high to make out its design.

"A planet carved to specification," the alien remarked. "Clearly a very advanced species."

"Maybe one not so wise," said Judith. "Nothing can grow on these surfaces, and it's not as beautiful as nature."

"It has mathematical beauty," Swaz defended. "It shows both rationality and an aesthetic sense."

"What about heart?" asked Judith. "You wonder how any beings live in in this world."

THE ALIEN DEMURRED its response and directed us to settle on the mountain side, upon

a crystalline formation that looked tetrahedral. "We made it," said the alien, as if it had been unsure that we would. "And they're here."

"Yes?" I questioned.

"They're not in our visible spectrum, but I can sense life forms. Quite a number..."

"Great, we can't see them. Can they see us?" asked Judith.

"Most likely, else they would not have gathered," said the alien. "This is going to be difficult."

"If we can't see them, we will not find out much," I added, wondering why I said the obvious.

"It could be because they have no dense bodily structures," considered the alien. "It means their consciousness is present in energetic forms only. Perhaps they are more evolved that I realized."

I wondered what it would be like not to have a physical space to retreat to. Then the alien, as if reading my thoughts, added, "They must have mental shields. I'm sensing high and low density areas, semi-shielded spaces."

"What about intent?" asked Judith. "Any sense of how they view us?"

"Unknown," replied the alien. "I think this is going to be as you earthlings say, 'Touch and go.'"

We weren't left wondering much longer, as an oval outline of pulsating energy appeared before us.

"I think it's a door. An invitation even," guessed the alien. "The question is, do we enter?"

"Time for another vote?" asked Judith

"What's the risk?" I asked.

"Remember, we have left our proper bodies behind," the alien answered. "And this would make us another step removed. This should be a unanimous vote"

"Would the aliens here seek our dying by invitation?" asked Judith. "If we go back without having discovered something more, we will be back to where we started and remaining there for an indefinite period. Still, it's like we are being led further out into the unknown."

"We have three days," I mulled.

"I concur this time," said Swaz. "It may be we have alter yet more to establish contact."

Judith guessed the problem. "We can assume the portal will take us somewhere, but how do we know we can come back?"

"Logically we don't," said Swaz. "Yet my vote remains to enter."

"Reason?" I asked.

"The captive confined space did not allow us to sense anything beyond it. One must risk death sometimes, in order to take the next step."

"Hmm, I considered. It was not an easy decision. I still considered myself somewhat the captain who had to consider the safety of his crew.

I finally agreed. "If we return to the cylinder, we turn down their invitation. Our best hope for ever leaving is establishing contact. So we should go."

I could tell that Judith was not happy, although she saw the logic. Too many unknowns did not mean you went further out on a limb. She did not bother to formally vote, her silence taken as tacit agreement.

"Are we ready?" asked Swaz, focused on the energetic opening.

"Yes," I replied for us.

"Portals are tricky, I should forewarn," said the alien. "There will be profound disorientation, like dying. Just ride it out. Don't fight it. Let the portal do the work."

"Sounds like a great experience," said Judith.

"We will make it out," said Swaz. "Be prepared. Something unexpected can be on the other end. Don't try to comprehend it all at once."

"Let's do it," I said, not wanting to talk anymore about it.

I looked at Judith, wondering if we would see each other again. She looked back at me, and I wondered if she had a similar fear.

The meld came apart as we passed, or so it seemed. The alien went first, then Judith and me. At first, utter blackness, then you sensed energy building. It built until it could build no more, and we were hurling toward infinity, or so it felt. It seemed it would have or could have no end. Surprisingly, I found it pleasurable, and wondered how long this feeling would last, when the meld returned.

We had stopped, opening our eyes to an aqua color around us, covering everything, even ourselves.

"What is it? Where are we?" I asked.

"Transitional space," informed the alien. "A while longer and things should take form."

It seemed like an eternity before it happened.

Suddenly heavy, a pulse of pain, and we fell upon the protrusions of a spongy surface.

I felt relieved at the sponginess, a hopeful sign of the organic.

We stood up, trying to maintain our balance. We looked around, finding ourselves in a new world and a glimpse which quickly faded, of entities or aliens with a greenish cast.

Chapter VIII
Classic Green Aliens

"I wouldn't have thought it possible," said Swaz.

We were all now looking down, feeling our legs, hands and arms. "I'm really here," said Judith, not fully believing it. "Touch me."

I reached out and grabbed her arms. "You're real as ever," I said.

"And you too."

"Unexpected," said the alien. "But perhaps not unpredictable. To transport in this portal must have required a full body. It could have, on the other hand, sundered us and ended things, but instead the portal joined us. It seems we had what you earthlings call luck."

The fact that we had gained our bodies distracted us from our surroundings, of which we quickly took stock. We were among growing things like plants, although they were geometric, from tetrahedral to geodesic forms, and instead of green, a mauve. The "plants" had alternate colors of orange and yellows near their tops, which were possibly flowers or reproductive structures.

"It's beautiful," said Judith. "And look over there."

We passed through the meadow and came upon a brook, where water flowed, a deep turquoise. We all drank, for our bodies had lacked hydration back in the cylinder.

"What next?" I asked Swaz.

"Over there!" it pointed.

We made out barely visible beings, luminescent with green and a hint of aqua. When they moved, they seemed to leave a brief after image of themselves in lighter color.

Swaz coloring had somewhat mirrored them, its skin toning to green.

Great," I said. "Classic green aliens."

The color seemed to be the most settled thing about them, for their shape wavered between appearing as an ethereal mirage and something more definite, yet even that remained uncertain.

"What are we seeing, Swaz?" I asked.

"Still determining. Contact is changing us too."

"Do these aliens have a set form?" asked Judith.

"One based on energetic fields," Swaz informed.

"It must have some material basis," Judith commented. "All life has bodies."

"I am only reporting what I see," Swaz replied. "There doesn't seem to be much body behind them, or at least one that's visible. It's possible that we're seeing digital creations, however. But I rather think they've tapped into a potentiality we have yet to discover."

"You mean they're more advanced?" I asked.

"You can say that," said Swaz. "Although advancements are usually paired with novel deficits."

"I can imagine that losing a body would be problematic," said Judith.

"It could make for a certain unpredictability..." Swaz agreed.

"Should we try to get closer?" I asked. "We'll be making contact, I suppose."

Swaz concurred. "I'm not sensing hostility."

We continued along the tetrahedral garden, splurged with colors. Our alien friend was now greyish green, as if simplifying. "You're coloring has gone down," observed Judith.

"It's best to stay neutral," said Swaz. "We don't know how our hosts interpret color."

Swaz's color drained even further, such that it looked like a grey albino, its baldness apparent, for before its head had wrapped it in darker color.

As they neared, Judith observed. "Interesting. They're coming in and out of our vision, moving, then disappearing."

"Their energetic patterns appear unstable to us," Swaz discerned. "Perhaps they're going in out of this world."

"To another world?" I asked.

"Perhaps the word is dimension, one related to this one but parallel," Swaz elaborated.

"Their dream world," said Judith.

As the three approached the energetic forms, a threshold was crossed when they saw more. The aliens appeared to have some bodily dimension, when the energy settled for an instant, before dissipating into green and yellow fringed energy. Then it would cycle again. There were at least four of these alien forms.

Although the energy did not seem to react to them, Judith commented, "It feels like they are watching intently."

"We're being noted," Swaz confirmed. "Fortunately, we are not deemed to be a threat to them, and they do not think it necessary to stop whatever they are doing."

The three stopped at a point when they felt resistance, an invisible barrier. This field of heightened energy was resistant and felt hazardous to enter.

"This is how close we are allowed to come," Swaz informed.

"We just watch?" I asked.

"We wait. Who knows how they perceive time. But there is some reason that we have come here and that they are present."

"I thought we escaped," said Judith.

"I think it was a test," said Swaz. "They're wondering about us and testing us as well."

Then, as if on cue, the green energetic fields embodied. Their size ranged from larger adults to smaller children, as they took near standard human form. We weren't sure if this was their selection to make themselves less threatening, or if it was their regular form. Nonetheless, we were grateful, for aliens with faces and bodies was less unsettling. Their bodies, however, retained the peculiar greenish cast, as energy shimmered on their surface. Their energy clothed them in a sense, also making us more comfortable.

Communication started, but neither Judith and I could interpret. Apparently our alien friend could. The green alien's mouths opened and changed shape, but the sounds not frequencies we could hear.

"It reminds me of elephants on earth who use low frequencies to communicate," said Judith. "But it's probably higher frequencies here. The course of mammalian evolution was to have a longer inner ear structure to pick up more frequencies.

"What are they saying?" I asked after a time, in which a lot of communication had transpired. Swaz's colors had come back some, mostly yellows, which I took as a good sign.

Our alien friend continued for a while longer, before addressing us. "It's as you say, 'There's good news and bad news.'"

"You might as well tell the bad news first," I said.

"The bad news is that there is no ship or mechanical means of transport off this planet, as they have no such technologies.

Judith interjected, "I suppose the good news is that they are not hostiles and want to help us."

"Close," said Swaz. "It's that and a little more. They are willing to train us in inter-dimensional travel, even though we are embodied."

"Is that possible?" I asked. "And are you sure we can trust them? Perhaps they wish to use us for their own purpose. As you've said, we know of no one who has returned."

"I don't think they need us for anything. As for trust, we are already entrusted to them. This is their planet and they know survival here."

"You're forgetting we were abducted," said Judith. "Was that necessary?"

"Reasonable question," said Swaz. "It turns out they have a code to be hospitable. When they saw a damaged ship passing, with only three persons present, they assumed we needed help. As for the green cone, it's as we suspected, a standard precaution. Not everyone, not even from stranded ships, are friendly."

"But they could have let us continue, and we would have been safe," I countered. "They didn't ask us."

"At the time I did not tell you that the ship had a number of inoperative sensors. I had chosen an optimistic interpretation of the data. There was a probability that would have run out of fuel, or been slung by a gravitational field to be left to drift in space."

"And they knew that?" asked Judith.

"Possibly. They revealed information, which could only have come from our ship. I believe they were able to do some rudimentary diagnostics. So it's possible they actually saved us."

"If they understand machines so well, why don't they build any?" I asked.

"We would have to ask them. My guess it's that they've moved away from machines to pure energetics, as with their bodies," said Swaz.

"So we're left with inter-dimensional travel," said Judith. "It sounds risky."

"Unknown," said Swaz.

A few moments of silence followed, then the aliens, who had slipped away, re-embodied to communicate.

"What are they saying, Swaz?" I asked.

"You may call me Solaris now," said our alien friend, "a more true name emerging after contact. Our alien friends want us to re-energize with them."

"What does that mean?" asked Judith.

"I think that means we are to eat. I'm not sure what food they could offer us."

The food was disappointing, hard capsule-like cylinders. No doubt it was what our bodies needed exactly, but absent the pleasure of eating and good cheer that normal food promotes. Nonetheless, there was entertainment, a light show of swirling energetic forms, like being immersed in a kaleidoscope.

Though no words transpired that we could understand, we were starting to read the green aliens' mood. They presented as even emotioned, with a pulsing, ecstatic undercurrent that could surface. This current would ebb and flow, but always return to the more evened state. I supposed it was by choice that they entered into this alternate state. Perhaps connected with this, our hosts would virtually disappear, then return in a transition state, somewhere between energy and body, the energy taking time to transform into matter.

Pretty soon we forgot about eating, and perhaps the aliens did too, for they ate only what was initially before them and nothing more.

Solaris, who had been absorbed in the alien contact, said, "I have good news; the aliens have discovered a way to contact you directly."

"Yes?" I said intrigued how the problem was resolved.

They can speak directly in your mind as a type of thought. Of course, you would have to grant permission, for it would violate their rules otherwise.

"I don't know if we should," Judith immediately said, although she knew they would end up accepting. "You can't survive if you can't communicate," was a basic rule, and it was especially true if you were in an alien world.

The link was established, although it took time. It came with increasing clarity as we responded to each other in thoughts. An unexpected thing was that I could read Judith's thoughts as well. They weren't actually worded thoughts, but its mood, intention, and general drift.

Are you sure you want to go through with this?" I asked Judith, when the link was about to become clear. "It's like we will be over-exposed."

"I suppose... But we will have to be careful with our thoughts."

"We can trust each other," I considered. "The problem is that the aliens will gain intimate access. We hardly know them."

"Or we could continue to use our alien friend as a go-between. But if we communicate directly, we'll come to understand them a lot better, which should enhance our survival."

"Life," I reflected. "You gain something, you risk something."

"Always," said Judith.

We made contact, and it was an expansion of consciousness that nearly overwhelmed us. We sensed the totality of things in this world and how they were connected.

"We're directly sensing fields now," said Judith. "Look at the living things."

Where before the plants had been geometrically surfaced, now radiating fields softened their outlines, with arcs of dotted energy.

"I didn't know plants had halo's," I commented.

"We all do now," said Judith.

Indeed, there was almost too much visible energy around us, which made us feel like we should look indirectly.

"Didn't know you had such a glow about you," I complimented.

"Yours is not bad either."

What was even more curious was when energy fields overlapped. It was at this point that we could read or feel the other's thoughts. Right now our mental frame was jumping around, dancing from the novelty of the experience.

We noticed the aliens that we could see through their green energetic domain more clearly. I found this paradoxical and asked Judith, "How is that we see their body better now?"

"I suppose because we more connected to the energetic fields. So the energy becomes clearer."

It was some relief to consider that the aliens might only "read" thoughts when they were within our fields."

"So as long as we don't get too close, we should have some privacy," I surmised.

"It may just be our limitation," warned Judith. "We should operate as if we are more transparent than we think."

"Fair enough," I replied.

I informed Solaris about our concern. His energy was more transparent as well, such that rainbows of fields danced around his body. We were relieved to find congruity between them and whatever he said.

"As to your concern, there's truth to both positions. The closer we are to the aliens here, the more accurate they can read us. At a visual distance, I surmise that they can still read the general cast and drift our thought. It's better not to be conspiring ill."

"What about random thoughts?" asked Judith.

"They will have less intensity. Unless will is behind them, they're likely to be background chatter. Nonetheless, a recurring thought would likely be noticed."

This reassured me some. Yet the whole matter was disconcerting, that we might need to close off portions of our being from ourselves.

"We'll have to have poker minds," I mused out loud.

"I suppose you are tiring from all this novelty," said Solaris.

It suddenly hit us. We had been awake since our new alien encounters and we needed sleep.

As if answering a question, Solaris informed, "This species goes into a reduced energy state for a relatively brief period, one that you would hardly notice."

"They're always awake?" wondered Judith.

"No. At least once in their day cycle they lose consciousness and their REM stage is heavily compacted. At this time the energetic field exhibits a different design."

"I see you've been studying them," I said. "So they may not have designated areas for us to sleep."

"My guess is that we will have to improvise," said Solaris. "I know you like protected spaces, so I have found an alcove."

After some communication by Solaris to the home planet aliens, we left their immediate presence and were led to a terraced area, curved like a bowl. Overhead an arched grotto shielded geometric, bulbous-like grass. It made for a comfortable cushion.

"You have done well for us," thanked Judith.

No sooner than we laid down, we fell asleep.

When we woke, we remembered our dreams, which were beautiful and disturbing. We had merged with the new aliens, such that our bodies became indistinct. The novel energy felt light and airy, like we had no weight, and no burdens with regard to the universe. It was freeing, but we were left wondering where our bodies had gone.

"Remarkable dream," I said. "And we had the same dream."

"The light floating feeling, I liked it so much," said Judith. "But the missing body was not so great. I think the dream is warning us, not to become too close to the aliens here. Yet, it would seem the closeness is also our path out."

So it was that we became better at it. We learned "phasing," how to feel our bodies as energy, where our body boundary would blur and we become more one with the environment or with whom we were communicating.

"Perhaps it's too advanced, stretching our evolutionary strings too taut," I opined after a session with the aliens.

"Yes, we're being pushed beyond our normal capabilities and awareness," Judith agreed. "The question is at what price."

"Do we become more advanced, or more true to our race?"

"Maybe that's it. We have a choice to make..."

We asked Solaris his opinion on the matter.

"In evolutionary change there are risks," he safely noted. "I think it depends on their intention."

"Yes?" we asked, waiting for more.

"The question remains: Are we being amplified as equals, or are we to be absorbed into their energetic matrix?"

"You mean, become part of a Borg?" asked Judith. "It doesn't feel that way. Rather, it's the opposite, like being released, expanding too much."

"We are dealing with an unknown," Solaris conceded. "To be safe, we should reserve a part of ourselves, don't go in all the way in. We always want to reserve the option to return."

"That makes sense. I'm partial to my body," I replied.

The next day it happened, the pull to a total merging. The alien presence was more powerful, a potency that went through every ripple of our bodies. It would take, it seemed just a feather weight more for us to be merged to a point of no return.

Chapter IX
Surveyor Ship

Commander Struck shook his head. The whole fleet taken and all life lost – not a few who were his friends—at least all, except possibly one ship that went off grid.

"Could one have gotten away?" he asked his scientific advisor.

Teron was part alien, part human, so he proved useful in understanding not only science but alien mentalities.

"That would seem to be the case, Commander. If the ship was destroyed, its black box signature would have sent confirmation. As it is, there was no signal at all. It would appear that a single survivor was on board, for records show that all space pods ejected from that zone, except one."

"Except one?" repeated Commander Struck. "It means we could have a lone survivor."

"Logically possible, but highly unlikely..." noted Teron. "For one, it is difficult to commander a ship alone, much less defend it." Supplies would be limited."

"Then perhaps that one was taken prisoner."

"Our enemies don't take prisoners in such situations."

"Still, we must look," said the Commander. "It's the code. I agree chances are remote."

"Let me first carefully review the records, before we put anyone at risk," requested Teron.

"Agreed," said the commander. "Look far beyond the initial point though. Let's assume he or she escaped."

Teron reported back the next day. "We've located the ship. It has been adrift in space for several weeks now."

"Adrift? Signs of life or power?"

"Neither."

"How far from the point of initial ejections?"

"Quite far, the ship was headed toward another bearing."

"In all likelihood, the survivor ran out of power and died. The ship is a coffin. It's quite sad," said the captain. "In what direction did the survivor go?"

"Toward Epsilon space."

"Not necessarily the best direction to go, even if you're escaping. It's considered highly dangerous."

"When one escapes, one does what is necessary."

"Yes, of course. But from one hostile power to another?"

"I would not say Epsilon is hostile. We have no record of their displaying aggressive actions."

"Perhaps it's not the right word. It's just that no one returns from there."

"That could mean different things. They could be unable to leave, or perhaps they are happy there."

The Captain laughed. "Yes, there are different logical possibilities."

"I assume there is no need to check on an adrift ship."

"No, check it out. Something about this is curious. I don't know quite what. And though the chances are small, the rewards could be great. The survivor could tell us how he survived, what really happened out there."

"Do we send the usual crew?"

"Yes. Put Delphi in charge. She has the highest find rate in the fleet. And Teron, I would like you to go too."

"Me, sir? You have not sent me out in the field for some time. What if a need arises here?"

Commander Struck laughed again. "Your junior officer needs some training. I need someone out there who I can trust will be able to handle a potentially difficult situation. We did a loose a fleet in an instant, and I don't want it to happen again. Plus, if one person survived, I want to know more about that person."

"As you wish, Commander."

"One more thing, Teron. I was thinking a small, but heavily armed ship."

"I respectively submit that we use a small but fast surveyor ship, only defensively armed. Speed is critical, rather than arms. We don't want to provoke hostility. And if something were to happen, they would only lose a few crew."

"I can't lose you," said Commander Struck. "So don't let that happen."

"I will keep that in mind," said Teron.

Commander Struck stepped away. He had lost some friends out there, and he wondered if one of them had survived. It was a long shot, but it was a loose end. And the Commander did not like loose ends.

Teron had a ranking higher than Delphi, but as commander of the ship, she would be in charge. Still, his suggestions would carry great weight, and he was friends of the commander.

She was surprised when he informed her that he would be joining them, and that the chance of achieving success was remote.

"Is there something I don't know about," she had queried.

"I have informed you of all that I have been told," said Teron.

Delphi had a sixth sense. "There's something more."

"I have my opinion on this matter, if that is what you mean. I know that logically there can be no survivors. And if there were any, it is highly unlikely they would be retrievable. Our first objective remains to stay alive."

"We must stay alive to complete the mission," allowed Delphi. "But if the commander makes a special request, I must complete it."

"You have always been determined. I think completion may be finding out what happened."

"The orders are find and retrieve. I'm bringing something back, even if it's bodies."

"Space is vast."

"We have coordinates of the ship. We will first go there. In all likelihood, we will find our answer or our first lead there."

Delphi went back to her quarters to rethink the situation. The drifting ship was in a delicate area. Not technically in Epsilon space, but close enough that they would be monitored. Delphi reviewed the ship logs that had gone near the system. For some reason the ships made the mistake of going near restricted space. The ones who had entered that near space before had recounted a strange energy emanation that was more mental than physical. *Perhaps it's like the Sirens of the Odyssey,* mused Delphi. *Something draws them in, and they don't return. What could it be?*

When she later conferred with Teron on the matter, he said, "I think I would be impervious to any attraction. I don't know about a full human."

"If you see me making decisions not to the benefit of this ship, you may take command," Delphi said.

"Do you really think that could happen?" asked Teron. "You are a woman of mission who rarely fails."

"I don't believe I would succumb. But a mission's success is often beyond any one person, and you are my backup."

"I am pleased to have your trust," Teron answered.

"It is not foolhardy. I have read your record. You were a fleet commander and to site one accomplishment, your maneuvers saved the planetary system in the second Quasar war. I know you are quite capable to handle a surveyor ship in a borderland area."

"I did not know that my biography had been declassified," wondered Teron.

"Commander Struck saw it fit to upgrade my clearance to the highest level."

Teron's eyebrows raised. "Perhaps he has an interest in you."

"Seriously Teron? Would he be sending me into death's way if he did? I think he has more interest in whoever might have survived out there.

The Commander would hear none of my objections about putting me in command," Delphi went on.

"He knows you're quite good at what you do, and you have more will than me."

"Usually I can put things together with the commander, but we will have to leave it there. We should be approaching the ship by the next earth cycle. Then we will know more of what we are up against."

It took a full two weeks to reach proximity to the ship. They were within scanning distance, approaching in stealth mode.

"No life forms, as expected," said Teron, viewing the read out.

"They steered the ship for some distance. It's possible someone is alive in the protective chamber."

"Yes, but there is no reason to be in there if they are not under threat. They could also have died or been captured."

"Captured? The ship looks intact, no sign of breaching."

"There is some other significant information."

Delphi waited

"There are faint pulses from the engine core."

"Meaning it's dormant and they could have gone further, but didn't."

That is correct," said Teron. "That argues for sudden stopping or being stopped. Possibly life support systems were used up."

"So we are going in for a look?" asked Teron.

"Yes. We have to start eliminating the possibilities."

"There's something more," said Teron, with a rare trace of puzzlement.

The pause was longer than usual and Delphi prodded, "Yes, what is it?

"There's some energy emanating in the 540–580 THz range, coming from the center of the ship."

"What does that mean?"

"It's an atypical signal. No known instrument of ours would produce that frequency."

"A breach by aliens?"

"Possibly a probe or actual presence."

"The plot thickens. We have found something after all. Anything more about that frequency? Is there something special to it?"

"I do not know," said Teron. "It's the frequency for teal green."

Chapter X
Greenwaves

For a time there was no contact with the Greenwaves as we came to call them. We almost forgot they were there. But they were still present, for we would be reminded by a green shimmering in the sky, in the water and places we did not expect.

I tried to imagine what it would like to be partially disembodied or not fully embodied and found it difficult. Normally we are not so conscious of our body unless something is wrong. But we had a body. So what would be like for waved aliens who were hyper-conscious and less conscious of any physicality? Was that state a natural evolutionary progression, or a dead-end path leading to extinction? How did that impact their moral nature? Were they good or bad, or had they discarded such categories, following unknown imperatives. The latter more readily described the feeling after our encounters and led me to be some disturbed. Additionally, Solaris would be inexplicably gone for extended periods. We supposed it was spending time with the Greenwaves, which only increased our fears.

"We don't know what is their end or what they're working toward," I remarked one day to Judith. We were resting in a rock alcove which gave us a sense of privacy.

"Maybe that is what Solaris is finding out," she suggested.

"Perhaps," I said, my tone conveying uncertainty.

"I suppose they are like all beings, in that they want to survive."

"Yes, but highly conscious beings will want more. The question is, what? Are they like humans? Do they seek power and control?"

"I sense they are different in that regard," intuited Judith. "I think they are more curious as to what makes other aliens tick, and they want us to stay until they figure that out."

"That could take our lifetimes. Perhaps they want to convert us to their kind?"

"Perhaps," said Judith. "Though it must take millennia to achieve that evolutionary state."

"If that's the case, they'll be waiting for us to have children."

Judith face did not have a pleasant expression, but she continued the thought. "So we are a new Adam and Eve, an experiment for their world?"

"Maybe this isn't their main world, and we've been placed in one of their auxiliary planets." I continued to muse.

For a while we drifted into reverie. To be founders of a planet was no small thing, surpassing anything we could do in our former world."

"The enticement must be great," Judith discerned. "To never see your family of origin again, to discard all past relationships for that. As they said, no one has returned."

"So they become founders of new worlds. To start history..."

"Yes, they wouldn't want it to be revealed to the outside, for such early worlds would be fragile. You have to give the Greenwaves credit though, if this is true. The Greenwaves don't make machines, but make worlds."

It was tempting, the idea, but there was something I didn't like about it. "Do we have a choice?" I wondered. "If they can make worlds like that, they could certainly send us home."

"Like you suggested, it may be their imperative."

"It would seem we would still have a choice. I think they would have grant it, in order for such worlds to be a success.

"Yes, when we almost became totally merged," Judith recalled.

I still don't remember what kept us from merging all the way..."

"Yes, something held me back. It was a memory," revealed Judith.

"Really?" I asked. "What was it?"

"I'll keep it private for now. If we manage to get off this world, I will tell you."

"We could ask their intentions directly," said Judith after a lengthy silence.

"Perhaps they already know our question. We don't know how well our thoughts are shielded here."

"Solaris is the key," I came back to. "If there is a way out, I would trust it to find the solution."

"You don't want to become a founder parent with me?" objected Judith with feigned rejection.

"You would make a fine parent. It's just that random pairings are more likely to become friends."

"I don't find many things random," Judith replied. "Still, I'm in agreement with you. Survival first, then our goal is to go home."

We raised our concerns to Solaris when he finally reappeared. Lately, his color was veering to shades of green, as if he was already beginning a transformation.

"Interesting hypothesis," he said without any elaboration, so we queried further.

"There are really two main questions," I summarized. "What do our hosts intend for us? And is there a way off of this planet?"

"I don't know if they have intentions per se," Solaris replied. "They are more like presenting us with their world and seeing what we will do."

"But suppose we want to be done with it?" asked Judith.

"They don't provide that mechanism, as a matter of course. They believe you should experience their world more fully before you would decide to leave."

"So that's an intention," I declared.

"A mild one then," granted Solaris. "But what you do with the experience, I believe they leave to you."

"So we can leave?"

"Yes. But no one has after the full immersive experience."

"We've resisted that, and we have a right to resist it."

"Perhaps that's an earthling stubbornness that they don't understand," suggested Solaris.

Judith's words surprised me next. "What harm can it be to learn more about their world? If we decide to go back, we would be providing valuable information about an unknown species. It may be something even critical to the survival of the universe."

"Survival of the universe?" I repeated. "That is the big picture."

Judith eyes sparkled, then seemed distant. "I sense there's a key here, a hidden key to the future. We've been losing battles lately. The other side has chosen disharmony, and it has been succeeding. We must stay and find out more."

I had no idea from what intuition she was drawing upon, yet her tone held certainty.

I went along with her hypothesis for the sake of coming to a conclusion. "That means to help save the universe, we have to fully know our hosts and whatever they have to offer, then have enough will power to leave. What no one else has ever done."

"Yes, we will be challenged," admitted Judith. "I wonder what the full merging would be like. It was god like, when we just approached it. Maybe, in this new-world mode, you become the god of that world."

"I think we're carrying this too far," I said. "But I have a feeling we would insult our guests if we don't imbibe their world more. I too sense there's something more we need to come to, before we leave this world, or before we'll be allowed to leave."

"So we stay?" asked Judith.

"Yes. So long as we don't start turning green..."

End of Part One

Did you love *Alien Ally*? Then you should read *Down Below and the Archon's Castle*[1] by Michael A. Susko!

[2]

In an underground fort, two children find a way to enter another world. There, they find friends in the form of a Sphere, a Rubbery Man and a Rock Man connected to the world below. The above world is controlled by an Archon, who collects aliens for exhibits. In this Wizard of Oz-like story, the children and their companions, battle the faceless thing that the Archon has become. Read this story to go on an archetypal voyage, the first of a seven-part series which follows the two children through their adult lives.

Read more at https://www.allroneofus.com/.

---

1. https://books2read.com/u/4Ax0YK

2. https://books2read.com/u/4Ax0YK

Also by Michael A. Susko

The Dreaming Series
Sleek Back
Streak and Cave Bear Dreaming
Moby and Marsupial Mole Dreaming

Worlds to the Side
Down Below and the Archon's Castle
Up Above and the Runaway
Across the Gulf and Journey Into Un-Time
On the Bay and a Wild Child Found
In the Wild and Do One Wild Thing
On the Mountain and Two Are Missing
To the Beginning and Journey Through Here

Standalone
The Little People
Animal Spell
Child of the Elements
The Firekeeper
Transformational Stories: Voices for True Healing in Mental Health

Caseness and Narrative: Contrasting Approaches to People Psychiatrically Labelled
Ten Pulses of Evolution & the Logarithmic Nature of Evolutionary Time
Street Images
Transformative Experiences, Psychiatric Research, and Informed Consent
Street Images II
The Lion and the Chameleon
Up Above and Down Below
Natural Extravagance and the Dynamic Vulnerability of Life
Flowers and Haikus
Alien Ally

Watch for more at https://www.allroneofus.com/.

About the Author

Michael Susko, with an M.S. in Counseling Psychology, taught in a progressive elementary school, which featured arts integration. He has designed and taught college classes on "Personal Archetypes" and "The Sacred Art of Indigenous Cultures." He has also led groups on dream interpretation, which explore how dreams can relate to everyday life. His familiarity with symbolism has helped him to write *Down Below*, which presents a fantasy realm which contains deep archetypal truths.

Read more at https://www.allroneofus.com/.